FERRY

The Jerusalem Cat

FERRY

The Jerusalem Cat

MARGHANITA LASKI

Illustrated by Meg Rutherford

ANDRE DEUTSCH

First published 1983 by
André Deutsch Limited
105 Great Russell Street London WC1

Photoset by
Rowland Phototypesetting Limited
Bury St Edmunds, Suffolk
Printed in Great Britain by
St Edmundsbury Press
Bury St Edmunds, Suffolk

ISBN 0 233 97529 2

*This book is dedicated
to my grand-daughters,
Esther Magdalen Godfrey
and Hannah Linet Godfrey.*

ACKNOWLEDGMENTS

For kindness that enabled me to write this book, I thank John Levy and the Friends of Israel Educational Trust who paid my fare to Jerusalem; Teddy Kollek, the Mayor of Jerusalem and his Committee who invited me to stay at Mishkenot Sha'ananim, and Ruth Bach and her staff who looked after me there; Pearl Silver and Joshua Prawer and Michael Avishai who each showed me some aspect of Jerusalem and its history; Fr. Eric Doyle, OFM, and M. P. Gardham of the Franciscan Study Centre at Canterbury for generous help; and Catherine Storr who advised me on the writing of children's books.

All the cats named in the present-day part of the story have been known to me. I am especially grateful to the original of Ferry who chose to live with me at Mishkenot, and to my own dear cat Sam Khan.

*   *   *

The picture of Jerusalem on the cover is adapted from a lithograph by David Roberts.

Once upon a time and not very long ago, a young black feral cat with blue-green eyes, and three white hairs hidden under his chin, was living on a stony hillside just outside Jerusalem. When the story begins, it was only a few months since this young cat's mother had turned him off to fend for himself, and he had not been fending very well. He had never had quite enough milk to drink, even when his mother looked after him, and now, when he had to look after himself, the best he could ever manage was only nearly enough to eat. So he was much too thin, and his coat was rough and rusty, and he was rather dirty because he never felt well enough to give himself a good lick all over; and his blue-green eyes, which should have been shining like aquamarines, were lack-lustre and dull. In those days, no one – no human – would have looked at him twice. In fact, no human had ever looked at him.

The only home this little cat had ever known was a patch of rough, weedy, stony ground just outside the Golden Gate in the high wall around the city of Jerusalem. Hardly a human ever walked there, for the Golden Gate has been closed for centuries and won't be opened, they say, until Doomsday, when all the dead will rise up and walk through it. So the only regular users of that patch of ground were the feral cats of the pack that our cat more or less belonged to, cats whose ancestors had long since gone wild, cats of all shapes and colours, and all of them always hungry. There was little enough food on that hillside for any cat to find and never enough for all of them, nothing but too few rats and mice, and in summer a few lizards, and once in a way perhaps a scrap of bread dropped by one of the Arab shepherds who pastured their goats on the slopes of Jerusalem's hill. But there were several other packs of wild cats living on the hillside around Jerusalem, with not enough food there for any of them, and woe betide any cat who ventured from his own pack's patch of ground on to another's.

The young cats who weren't yet any good at hunting and fighting came off worst, and our young black cat came off very badly indeed, because, though he was quite good at hunting, he was very bad at fighting. Then the other feral cats were, as they needed to be, frightened of almost everything so that they could be quick at spotting any possible kind of danger, and most of all they were terrified of human beings, for almost the only kind of human beings they came across were ones who would as soon as not throw stones at cats, just to amuse themselves.

But our young black feral cat – his name is going to be Ferry and he might as well be called by it now – Ferry was not really very frightened of human beings; not frightened enough for his own good, the other feral cats might well have said. And there was one kind of human being he wasn't frightened of at all, a kind who occasionally took a short cut across the cats' patch of hillside, and this kind was men who wore long brown woollen robes and sandals. Why the cat Ferry shouldn't have been frightened of such people he couldn't know and nor could he know that his mother had been just the same. But if his mother had been able to tell stories to her kitten, as human mothers do to their children, then this is what the cat mother would have told her son.

'There is a story in our family,' she would have told her kitten, 'and I had it from my mother, and she had it from *her* mother, and so on back for more than five hundred years. And the story goes that it was because of these men in long brown woollen robes and sandals that our family came to live in Jerusalem. These men were Franciscan friars, and our great-great-hundreds-of-times-great-grandmother was brought here by a Franciscan friar called Brother Paul.

'This Brother Paul had been living in a monastery in Italy, when he was told, one day, that he must take ship from Italy to the Holy Land, to the port of Jaffa, two days' journey from Jerusalem. The reason that Brother Paul had been sent for was that he was a very good cook. The Franciscan friars had several friaries, and one of the most important was their house just outside Jerusalem. In it there lived twenty-four Franciscan friars. One of their duties there was to give food and lodging to as many as they could of the Christian priests and monks and friars who came to the Holy Land in their hundreds every year, as pilgrims to the Holy Places of Christendom; and the most important duty of the Franciscans in the Holy Land was to look after the Holy Places. It was, and still is, the Franciscans who look after the church that was built over the stable in Bethlehem where Jesus was born, and who

help to look after the Church of the Holy Sepulchre in Jerusalem built over the places where, as the stories go, Jesus was crucified and buried.

So with such weighty responsibilities, it was essential that the Franciscans' house in Jerusalem should have a good cook. Brother Peter, the cook before Brother Paul, was an old man now who was going back to Italy to spend his last days in peaceful retirement. Brother Peter had come to Jaffa to go back home on the same boat that had brought Brother Paul, and before they parted he told Brother Paul:

'Our house in Jerusalem is a very good house, and our

cellarer, Brother Simon, who looks after the guests and the stores, is a very good cellarer who looks after the wines as they should be looked after and provisions me well enough in the kitchen; though I have to admit to you that he's a bit of a grumbler and more ready to see the dark side than the bright one. Still, you'll be glad to hear that the kitchen is a very good kitchen and well fitted with all that is needful, with a good herb garden just beside it. In fact, so far as the cook is concerned, there is only one thing wrong with our house in Jerusalem, and this is that as well as the friars who live there, and the

pilgrims who come and stay there, it is the home of hundreds and hundreds of mice and quite a few rats who scamper into the kitchen at night and eat up our provisions.

'But haven't you a good cat?' asked Brother Paul, and Brother Peter shook his old white head, and said sadly that the friary had no good cat, no cat at all. In fact, he said, he didn't believe there were any good cats, any true domestic cats in Jerusalem, only the feral cats who lived in the wild stony places and caught only the mice and rats they found on the hillside, and had nothing to do with any human beings at all.

Oh, dear, Oh dear, Oh dear, said Brother Paul to himself, this will never, never do. As there are no good cats up at Jerusalem, clearly I must take one there. But how was he to find one? As he walked through the narrow alleyways of the port of Jaffa, he could see that all the town cats were half-starved and half-wild, belonging to no one, running away from people, certainly not the kind of cats who would settle down to work in a friary. However was he to find a good hard-working domestic mouser to take up to Jerusalem?

Now in those days – so the mother cat would have told her black kittens – the Holy Land belonged not to the Christians or to the Jews, but to the Arabs. The Arabs had the same God as the Christians and Jews, and his name to them was Allah; But unlike the Christians, they didn't believe that God had a son. The Arabs believed, like the Jews, that Jesus was one of the prophets, but not the son of God. Only, unlike the Jews, they trusted even more in a prophet called Mohammed who lived six hundred years after Jesus, and founded the Moslem religion which the Arabs follow. The Moslems believe that their prophet Mohammed, at the end of his life, was standing in Jerusalem when he was taken up to Heaven alive. So they have built a mosque with a great golden dome over the place in Jerusalem where they believe this happened and this is a Holy Place to them – in fact, in all the western world there is no city so full of Holy Places as Jerusalem, for Christians and for Moslems and for Jews. But in Brother Paul's day, there were very few Jews in Jerusalem, for they had all been turned out of the country by the Romans soon after Jesus was crucified, fourteen hundred years earlier. Nor, apart from the friars, were there any Christians living in the country then. But the Arabs, who had let the friars come to look after the Christians' Holy Places, also allowed bands of Christian pilgrims to come and see the Holy Places and say their prayers there.

But there were several Arabs on the road from Jaffa to Jerusalem who hated Christians and would throw stones at the pilgrims as they went by, and sometimes attack them and rob them, and even kill them. So usually the Christians who wanted to travel on the road would pay friendly Arabs to look after them and see that they had a safe journey.

The Arab who was looking after the Franciscans at the time of Brother Paul's arrival was a merchant of Jaffa called Idris, and when Brother Paul discovered that there were no good mouse-hunting cats to be found in Jaffa, he asked Idris if there was any possible hope of his finding one anywhere.

'You have asked just the right man at just the right moment,' said Idris. 'Six months ago, my ship-captain brother arrived with a cargo of goods from Tangiers in Morocco, which is where my family comes from. Our eldest brother is a doctor there, and he sent me by this ship one of our own family's beautiful cats, undoubtedly the most beautiful cat that has ever been seen in the Holy Land, a shining black cat with bright blue-green eyes, and the most wonderful mouse-catcher I have ever known, even in this family of exceptional mouse-catchers. My daughter has named her Sultana, because she is as beautiful and as dignified as a sultan's chief wife. Three months ago Sultana bore four kittens, and they are just now ready to leave her. One of them I will sell to you.'

'Oh dear, oh dear, oh dear,' cried Brother Paul. 'One of your Sultana's kittens sounds just what I want. But I can't buy one, in fact I can't buy anything, because I am one of the friars of St Francis who have promised God that we will always be poor and use money only to help other people. But,' he added earnestly, 'our founder Francis loved all animals, and any cat that came to live with us would have a good home.'

Idris laughed. 'I am sure of that,' he said, 'and when I said I would sell you a kitten, I didn't mean that you should pay with money. You're a cook, aren't you, and if there's one thing I enjoy more than another, it's a good meal. So I will sell you a kitten for the best meal you can cook me after we arrive in Jerusalem.'

'Agreed!' said Brother Paul joyfully, and straightaway he and Idris went off through the narrow alleys to Idris's fine house, built round a courtyard and protected by high walls and a great iron-barred wooden gate. On one side of the courtyard were the stables; and there, in a manger on a piece of goatswool carpet, lay the shining black mother cat, Sultana, fast asleep, with her big, plump kittens asleep between her paws.

There were four of them. One was black. One was black with a white nose and shirt front and white paws. One was sandy-grey with blackish stripes, and one was a tabby. And as Brother Paul looked at them and wondered however he should choose between them, the black kitten rolled over and opened the brightest blue-green eyes Brother Paul had ever seen in a cat. It stared straight at him and then it stretched out its neck as if inviting Brother Paul to tickle it under its chin, where, he could see, there were three thick white hairs.

'I'll have the black kitten with the aquamarine eyes,' said Brother Paul without any more hesitation, hurriedly adding, 'If you please,' which he had forgotten in his excitement at finding what he felt sure was just the right cat. Idris smiled, then he picked up the black kitten by the scruff of its neck and dropped it into Brother Paul's hands. 'You have made the right choice,' he said. 'My little girl tells me that this black kitten is the best of the bunch and I know that it is, because it has the family looks.' Then he called out in Arabic (which Brother Paul couldn't speak yet) to one of his servants, and the man came running with a basket and another remnant of goatswool carpet.

'We'll let your cat travel on the bed he is used to,' said Idris, 'and then, until he gets to know you, he won't feel

so strange.' Gently, he tipped Sultana and her kittens on to the fresh piece of carpet. Then he took the old piece and put it into the bottom of the basket, and Brother Paul put the kitten there. All the way up the hills to Jerusalem Brother Paul held tightly to the basket with one hand while he gripped the saddle of his donkey with the other, and when the caravan stopped for meals, Brother Paul would take the little cat out of the basket and give him a good share of whatever food was going, and then tickle the little cat under his chin and stroke him till he fell asleep as he purred.

'What are you going to call your little cat?' Idris asked Brother Paul when the pilgrim caravan stopped for the night at Ramle, and the pilgrims had dismounted and were sitting thankfully round the fire. 'Such a fine cat deserves a fine name,' Idris urged, but Brother Paul who, like the other pilgrims, was sore and aching with the jolting donkey-ride, replied, a bit testily, 'Not a bit of it. He's going to have the simplest name a cat can have. For,' he went on, 'it doesn't become a mendicant cat to have a fancy name in case his master came to think too much of him and look on him as a pet and not a humble working beast.' Idris smiled to himself in the darkness, for he could see that Brother Paul was feeling a bit ashamed of growing so fond of his cat. 'Well, what are you going to call him,' he said, and Brother Paul said primly, 'I am going to call him Gatto, which in my language means simply Cat, a male cat, a cat who is a son, a brother, a husband, a father.' 'And Gatto,' the mother cat would have said to her son Ferry, 'was our ancestor's name for the rest of that cat's life, the name of the first cat of our family to live in Jerusalem.'

On the evening of the day after they had started from Jaffa so the mother cat would have continued, the caravan arrived at Jerusalem, and if Brother Paul was glad to get off his donkey and stretch his aching limbs, this was nothing compared with the delight of the hostel friars, at greeting Brother Paul, and especially the delight of Brother Simon, the cellarer, though from his grumpy manner you would never have known it. For since the old cook had left, Brother Simon had been preparing the meals, and the friars and the pilgrim priests who were staying at the hostel swore he was the worst cook in creation.

That first night Brother Paul was too tired to do more than attend the evening Vespers service and then stumble back to his cell, where he had left Gatto with a saucer of sheep's milk, and fall asleep on his pallet bed with the sleeping cat at his feet. Next day Brother Paul slept late, for the Guardian (which is the name of the head of a Franciscan friary) had said he was not to be disturbed. The sun was already high in the sky when he woke, much refreshed, and made his way to the kitchen, with Gatto trotting beside him. There he found Brother Simon with a group of food pedlars bargaining for the day's stores.

'Oh, there you are!' said Brother Simon in his grumpy way. 'I was beginning to think you'd sleep till Doomsday,' and then he saw Gatto, and said suspiciously, 'What's that beast doing here?'

'That is Gatto, the friary cat,' said Brother Paul. He had decided that a firm line from the start was the best way to get Gatto accepted as a member of the community. 'He has come up from Jaffa to clear the friary of mice, and,' he added cunningly, 'when there are no mice eating our food, you will need to spend much less money.'

Brother Simon couldn't but see the sense of this, yet it wasn't in his nature to speak cheerfully, so he just said darkly, 'Well, so long as he *does* work . . . I've taken a piece of our salted pork out of the barrel for you to cook for supper tonight,' he said. 'It's not very smelly yet, and there are plenty of herbs in the garden to cook it with, and if there's anything else in particular you want, you'd better have a look and see if these pedlars have it.'

'There's one thing I do want,' said Brother Paul, 'and that's a nice plump chicken to cook for Idris the merchant. I've invited him to supper in the kitchen tonight, and being a Moslem he won't eat pork.'

'Fancy you knowing that,' said Brother Simon, with reluctant admiration, 'but you can't go having private banquets with special food in the kitchen, you know. I don't know what our Guardian will say to that.'

'I'll go and ask him,' said Brother Paul, and off he went, leaving the cat and the cellarer looking distrustfully at each other. Soon Brother Paul came back, to say happily that the Guardian had said it would be all right, just this once, since the friars owed much to the goodwill of Idris the merchant. 'And,' added Brother Paul, 'it would be very nice, Brother, if you would eat with us too,' an invitation that Brother Simon accepted in his grudging way though secretly he was pleased to be asked; more pleased than Brother Paul was to be asking him, which he had done only because the Guardian had told him to.

All the rest of that day such delicious smells began to float out of the kitchen that everyone, friars and pilgrims, could think of nothing but the evening meal. And all that day, Gatto slept on his mat on the floor by the stove, and every time Brother Simon came into the kitchen, he would mutter, 'I wonder when that cat's going to start working.' But mostly Brother Simon kept away, because even he had the sense to know that a cook is best left to himself in his own kitchen, and Brother Paul just got on with his cooking and let Gatto sleep, knowing that most cats prefer to do their hunting at night.

What Brother Paul served that evening to the friars in their refectory and to the pilgrims in their dining room was a savoury dish of pork and beans flavoured with the delicious herbs he had found planted in the little garden beside the kitchen – sage and thyme and mint and oregan – not to speak of the spices – cinnamon and mace and nutmeg and cloves – that he had bought from the pedlars, all tongue-pricking tastes which the good cooks of those days would mix together in cunning ways to cover up the taste of the meat that had, as often as not, gone a bit off. But for the even better chicken dish that Brother Paul prepared for Idris and Brother Simon and himself, he used just a few of the right herbs and no spices at all, for the chicken was fresh and young, and the sauce he mixed to go with it was, as he remarked to the still-sleeping Gatto when he tasted it, 'as good a sauce as I've ever made, though I say it myself.'

So his guests said too, and with great enthusiasm,

when he put their plates on the table before them. And as he lifted the meat from the cooking pot and the good smells came rolling out, Gatto got up and stretched himself, and walked over to Brother Paul, then stood up on his hind legs and patted gently at his master's knee.

It was quite plain what he was asking for, and Idris wasn't in the least surprised when Brother Paul put some scraps of the chicken in a small brown bowl, tapped the bowl with his fingernail and then set it down on the floor in front of Gatto who eagerly tucked in. But Brother Simon said sourly, 'If you feed a cat, Brother, he won't bother to catch mice. Everyone knows that.'

Brother Paul looked taken aback, but Idris said firmly, 'These cats are different, Brother, as you will find. They are true domestic cats, house cats, and they take pride in keeping their homes clean of rats and mice. But you have to feed them and feed them well, because they never eat what they catch. They seem to look on rats and mice as vermin, just as we do.'

Brother Simon laughed and said, 'Then it's lucky your cat has a home to live in, for he'd never make out on the hillside here, where the wild cats eat all they catch, and glad to.'

Idris looked anxious. 'Indeed then, I hope Gatto never has to live out on the hillside,' he said, 'for one family of cats is as different from another as chalk is from cheese, and the cats of Gatto's family would be no good at living wild, no good at all, being gentle and loving and needing their humans as much as their humans need their cats.'

'I promise you,' began Brother Paul earnestly, 'I promise you that as long as I live . . .' and then he broke off, for what he saw was Gatto walking heavily towards the table, and in his mouth, a dead rat almost as big as himself which he laid down at Brother Paul's feet in recognition of the fact that this man and no other was his loved master. Before the evening was over, and Idris had let out the great big belch which is the polite Arab way of showing you have enjoyed your food, Gatto had brought along one after the other, four mice as well as the rat, and it might as well be said here and now that within a month of his arrival, and young as he was, Gatto had completely cleared the monastery of rats and mice, and kept it clear thereafter, with an occasional bit of hunting in the monastery gardens and on the very nearest bit of hill-side, just to keep his paw in practice.

It was about a year after Brother Paul and Gatto had arrived at Jerusalem that Brother Simon one day arrived in the kitchen with that look of glee in his face that is peculiar to ill-tempered people who bring unwelcome news. 'What is it, Brother?' asked Brother Paul uneasily, for he could see that something was up. 'Have you looked at Gatto lately?' asked Brother Simon ominously, and Brother Paul answered, 'Why no, Brother, not specially, that is to say. Why do you ask?' 'Well, I happened to notice him walking in the garden this morning –', said Brother Simon, and then he broke off and pointed to Gatto who had just stalked into the kitchen. 'Look, Brother Paul,' he said. 'Look for yourself.'

Brother Paul looked. Then he said, 'Oh dear, Oh dear, Oh dear.' For what he had seen, and should have seen quite a time before if he wasn't so used to Gatto as to take

him for granted, was that the name he had chosen for his cat had proved unsuitable. For it was absolutely clear that Gatto was not a cat who was a son and a brother and might one day be a husband and a father. Gatto was, and had been all along, a cat who was a daughter and a sister and a wife and about to be a mother. Gatto was a female cat who was very soon going to have kittens.

'That's not a very nice thing to happen, is it?' snapped Brother Simon. 'A female cat about to kitten in a friary where it's absolutely improper for females to be. You'd better change her name to Gatta, and turn her out of doors.'

Brother Paul – to his own surprise for he was normally the mildest and gentlest of men – found himself shouting. 'I shall do nothing of the sort. Gatto the cat was called and Gatto the cat shall be, whether he or she. And whether he or she, no follower of Saint Francis would turn an animal out of doors, and what happens when Gatto kittens is something we shall have to see.' Brother Simon slank away before Brother Paul's anger and took his story to the Guardian, but the Guardian said that Brother Paul was quite right, and at the first opportunity sent Brother Simon away to Italy.

When the time came for her kittens to be born, Gatto behaved so beautifully as to cause the least possible embarrassment to everyone. She took herself off to the old drainhole through the walls, which was her usual way of getting out to the hillside, and there she bore her first litter of kittens and the several more litters she was to have in the years to come, though only in the first litter, and never again thereafter, did Gatto bear a kitten who looked exactly like herself, black all over with aquamarine eyes and three thick white hairs under her chin. And Brother Paul, who now knew perfectly well what was going on, would tiptoe down with Gatto's own bit of carpet so that she and her kittens could lie soft, and with regular bowls of milk and tasty food. For as long as it took her kittens to open their eyes and grow up and be able to fend for themselves, Gatto lived with them in the old drain and never went near the friary at all. Then one day she would stand up and stretch herself and push the kittens away on to the hillside and then stroll back to the friary as though she had never left it, perfectly confident that that evening she would find her rug and her brown bowl of sheep's milk waiting for her in their usual places beside the cooking stove.

For many years Brother Paul and his Gatto lived together in Jerusalem in perfect love and amity, and when Gatto at last died, an old cat who had had a loved and happy life, Brother Paul said over her grave in the herb garden, 'You have had the best death for a cat, which is to die before its master. But this is sad, it is very sad for me,' and he turned and went away, and soon afterwards the Guardian sent him back to Italy, and there, not long after, he died too.

'And so,' the mother cat might have ended, 'Brother Paul was able to keep the promise he had made to Idris, that Gatto should never be turned out on to the bare hillside to fend for herself. But he could promise nothing for Gatto's descendants for he did not know then that there would be any, and so all of us, even those of us who are descended from that first-litter kitten who looked just like Gatto, and just like you, even we have had to try to make out on vermin and scraps. And just as Idris told Brother Paul, none of us is very good at it, and I am afraid,' she might well have finished, 'that you, my son, whom I am just going to push away from me for ever, as is our custom – you won't be very good at it either.' And she would have been right.

*   *   *

Of course, cats can't really tell their kittens what they've learned from *their* mothers and *their* mothers from *their* mothers and so on back for perhaps hundreds of years.

But what they can do and do do is to show their children what they themselves have learnt, and sometimes the lessons they teach may not be the most useful ones for a changed way of life. Ferry had learnt to stalk his prey and then leap on it more quickly and cleverly than any other cat in the pack; no rat or mouse or lizard could get away from him, once he had decided to catch it. But when he had caught it, he would never eat it right away. Instead he would pick it up in his teeth and stand looking around for a moment, as if there was somewhere – or someone – he wanted to take it to rather than eat it. Naturally, the other cats had learnt to wait for that moment, and, as often as not, when Ferry did at last decide he'd better eat his catch, he found that some other cat had snatched it away. More than once he had been nicked by a stone thrown at him by a boy because he'd stood and looked hopefully at the boy, instead of running as soon as any boy came near; and when at last Ferry did run away, more than once he'd run straight into a big stone, because his training hadn't been so strongly on running away as on giving him a feeling that he oughtn't to be running away, that running away from humans was something he shouldn't need to do at all.

So taking all in all, Ferry was far from being the best-fed cat in that tribe of ill-fed cats on the mountain, though the first months of his living on his own had not been too bad. He had been born in the late winter of a good year when the weather had been gentle, and after his mother had turned him out, there were enough rats and mice and sometimes young birds about to keep him going, despite what the other cats stole from him. Then that year it was rainy on and off, right up to the late spring, and this was good weather for homeless Jerusalem cats, for the rain made the grass grow on the hillside under the walls, and the mice who ate the grass seeds flourished and were plentiful.

But after that good spring the sun began to shine, and it shone every day and all day and ever more hotly. The sun dried up the grass and so the mice soon vanished from the rough bare slopes. It was a painful, and terrible year for cats with no homes to go to. The sun went on shining, and the skies were deep blue, and the pilgrims and tourists who came to Jerusalem from all over the world said, 'What beautiful weather!' But for most of those who dwelt in and around Jerusalem the weather was not beautiful but cruel: for the men and women and children who had to work in the great heat of summer; for the plants and trees that had to survive with no fresh water to drink; for the homeless animals who could find almost nothing to eat.

That year the hot dry summer lasted well into what should have been autumn, and after it, with almost no mild weather in-between, came one of the harshest, coldest winters that Jerusalem had known for many years. For the small black cat Ferry it was his first winter, and it was, very nearly, his last. He was not yet a year old when the snow began to fall, and for the tiny scraps of food that could still be picked up by the half-wild cats, he hadn't much of a chance. He was so thin now and so weak that he had no weight to bring to bear in pushing against bigger cats: in any case, to fight for his food wasn't in his nature. All the other cats on the hillside were ready almost to scratch each other's eyes out for any scrap of food, scrunching up their backs, hissing and biting and clawing. Ferry had got used, now, to having his mice snatched away from him unless he was – for him – unusually quick in eating them. But even if he found food, like a crust of bread that a child had let fall, Ferry would always allow another cat – and there always was another cat – to share it with him. This, too, must have been something he learned from his mother and she from her mother, and so right back to Gatto who had never had to fight for food.

But such courteous, such polite behaviour doesn't

help a thin little cat to live on a Jerusalem hillside through a harsh winter, and if anyone had looked at Ferry then (but no one ever did), they would have said, 'If that little cat doesn't get a square meal soon, he won't have long to live.' All the cats on the Jerusalem hillside were in a bad way, but Ferry was in one of the worst. For weeks now there had been almost nothing for any cat to eat, and least of all for him.

Then there came a day in that cold December when, as evening fell, a new smell, a hopeful if horrible smell, was wafted to the noses of Ferry's tribe of cats. It was the smell of carrion. And even Ferry, starving as he was, backed up a little and shuddered when the first wave of the horrible smell of rotten food came to him, as if with some memory of days when cats like him didn't need to eat food like that.

But those days were gone, and Ferry did indeed need to eat stinking carrion meat, to eat any food at all, if he was to stay alive. So Ferry began to crawl, stealthily, cautiously, for fear of the unknown dangers that always lurked, towards the horrible but hopeful smell. And so did the rest of his tribe.

What the smell came from was an old, old goat, one from the many herds of goats that their Arab owners grazed on the hillside, a goat so very old that he had just toppled over and died, and the reasons the cats hadn't found the body earlier were both that it lay among some ancient stone ruins where they wouldn't usually look for food, and that the wind was blowing the smell away from them. Now the wind had changed, and now the dead goat was nothing but meat, stinking life-giving meat, enough meat for all the tribe of cats. As they closed in on the meat, even little Ferry, with no weight to help him in the pushing and shoving, managed to get in a bite and was just about to take another when . . .

Suddenly, from round the side of the hill, there tore upon the cats a pack of wild dogs. Those dogs were as hungry as the cats, and they were bigger and fiercer, and if they could kill a cat and eat it, then that cat was only so much meat for them, and fresh meat too. Never in his whole life had Ferry been so frightened, so stiff, so frozen with fright. There he was, just about to take his second proper bite of food for weeks, when just above his head he heard a yapping and a growling and looking up saw a slavering mouth of teeth that were just about to snap, not on the stinking meat, but on *him*.

The other cats, the older cats who had met the wild dogs before, had backed away and stood there in a half-circle, yowling with stiff, arched backs. All they could hope for now was that something might be left on the old goat's bones after the dogs had eaten and slunk back to the Judaean hills where they lived and hunted until hunger drove them to the city. All the cats watched and waited, angrily, frushing their tails except for Ferry. He had been too hungry to hear the dogs come, too hungry to lift his head quickly enough, then too petrified with fright to move. Now, it seemed, in one minute, in one second, he himself was to be killed for food for a starving dog.

It was instinct for life, it was knowing that an animal has to do all it can to live, that made Ferry, at the very last possible moment, gather all the little strength he still had into a ball of ragged fur that leapt and touched ground and straightened out and began to run; to run madly, wildly, as the cat Ferry had never run before, to run and keep on running though he didn't know where to, only that he must go on running until he reached somewhere – if there was, in his whole world, anywhere – that felt safe. He ran right down the stony hill, right down to the bottom where he had never been before, and right on to and somehow over the road that encircles Jerusalem's hill. It was a miracle he wasn't killed, crossing that road, for the day was getting up now, and the road was crowded with bicycles and buses and lorries and cars carrying people going to work. But somehow Ferry ran between them all, while the drivers and riders cursed him, and still he ran on, over rough ground again now, and up a hill.

The dogs had given up the chase at the roadside and gone back to the carrion, but this Ferry didn't know. He was too mad with fright to know anything except that he must run and keep on running. Uphill he went, and now it was over soft ground, and now it was over hard ground, not hard and rocky but hard and smooth, and then suddenly there loomed up before him what was surely an enormous stone, a stone bigger than any stone he had ever seen before. He knew from experience now that if he wasn't to hurt himself he must swerve away from big stones, but the stone was so enormous and the swerve the exhausted Ferry was able to make was so much too small, that his mad run ended with him knocking himself silly by banging his head on what wasn't a big stone at all, but a perfectly ordinary English windmill –

ordinary in everything except in standing on a hillside opposite the city of Jerusalem.

*   *   *

Just around the windmill from where Ferry lay stunned, an old man was sitting in a folding canvas armchair. In his lap he held a silver flute. Behind him was a cage in which stood a large Victorian travelling carriage. In front of him, on a camp stool, was a young man, drawing him.

'But why, William,' the old man had just been saying, 'why, when you never paint anything but faces, do you

want to make your drawings of me with my flute in my lap, looking over the valley towards Jerusalem, and with a carriage in a cage behind me and a windmill by my side? And what, in any case, is a carriage doing here in a cage with a perfectly ordinary English windmill standing beside it?'

'That's a lot of questions, Ezra,' said William, blurring a line on his pad with his thumb, 'but I'll try to answer them, if only to keep you interested and reasonably still. First, then, it's *because*, as you rightly say, I paint only faces, that I like to draw the people I am going to paint with as much in their faces as possible. I don't want to draw people in my studio, even if it were possible and often it isn't, because I take my subjects wherever in Israel I find them, and not only in Jerusalem. But if I did take people to my studio, and when I first started that's what I often did, then I found their faces weren't nearly so full of what interested me as when I drew them where they belonged.'

'But I don't belong here,' said the old man, 'I don't really belong anywhere, except in Switzerland where I now live and in concert-halls anywhere in the world when I am playing my flute.'

'Fair enough,' said William. 'But I don't want to go to Switzerland to draw you, and I did go to your concert here last night and make some sketches. And it seems to me that to sit you down here with the carriage and the windmill, with the flute and the sight of Jerusalem, is perfectly fitting and should bring out the best in your face, as I can already see it will.'

'Jerusalem I can understand,' said Ezra. 'The flute I can

understand. But why the carriage and the windmill?'

'Because,' said William, then he broke off and said, 'Did you see something run behind me? Something black?' 'No, nothing,' answered Ezra, 'but then I was looking at Jerusalem – and how beautiful it is, Jerusalem the golden.'

The painter shrugged. 'Oh well, I don't suppose it was anything much. I just got a glimpse out of the corner of my eye,' and he sketched intently on.

'The carriage and the windmill, please, William,' said Ezra patiently.

William said, 'I chose to sit you by them because you are a Sephardi Jew. A Spanish Jew.'

'Now,' said Ezra, 'I have heard everything. It is true that I am a Sephardi Jew, which is a Jew from one of the families who used to live here in Jeruselem before the Romans turned us out. It is true that many of us went to Spain and therefore Sephardi Jews are often known as Spanish Jews. It is also a fact that at about the time that Christopher Columbus went to America we got turned out of Spain – poor Jews, we are forever being turned out, just like the poor gypsies. That time of turning out, my own family went with several other Sephardi families to what is now called Yugoslavia, and to a town where we all spoke and went on speaking such perfect Spanish that young Englishmen who wanted to become diplomats used to be sent to our town to learn the most perfect Spanish that was still spoken anywhere in the world.'

'Not any more?' said William softly, not quite a question. He knew what the answer would be, but he wanted the sadness spoken of before he told the story of the carriage and the windmill.

'Not any more,' agreed Ezra. 'The Nazis came. I was a very young man then – I am not as old as I look now – and I was at home with my family for the Passover when the Nazis came. They took us all: my father and my mother, my brother and my sister, my old grandmother who lived with us. They took all the Jews in our town, except for a very few of the young people who managed to flee to the mountains. They took us all to Hitler's concentration camps, some in Germany, some in Austria, some in Poland, and there, so far as I know, every one of us died – died from overwork and starvation or died in the gas chambers – every one of us but me.'

He paused, his eyes fixed very firmly on the golden city. 'You will ask, William, why I did not die and I will tell you. It was because of my flute. When they took us, I had my little flute in my pocket as I always did and always do, and when I could, I would play it to myself for – no, not for comfort, but to stay alive, as a man dying of thirst must drink. It happened that one day the Commandant of the German camp I was in heard me playing, and he kept me alive to amuse him and his officers with a bit of music whenever they felt like it, as if I were a monkey on a barrel organ.' His face twisted in disgust, and William kept silent, only intently moved his pencil. Ezra's face relaxed. 'Then the Germans were defeated and the Swiss Red Cross came to our camp, and thanks to one of their officers who loved music, I was able to go to music school in Switzerland. Now I am a Swiss citizen and I have my own music school there, and it is, as you know, my music school which has done me the honour of asking you to paint my portrait to hang in their concert hall.'

'The honour is mine, and theirs,' said William courteously and sincerely, 'because you are the best flautist in the world.'

Ezra was smiling a little now. 'That is as it may be,' he said. 'But we have come a long way from the story of the carriage and the windmill. Shall we go back to them now?'

'By all means,' agreed William. 'Well, then, the carriage belonged to Sir Moses Montefiore. The windmill was built by the orders of Sir Moses Montefiore. And Moses Montefiore was a Sephardi Jew like you, but an English Sephardi from one of those families that went to the north when the Spaniards turned them out, and eventually settled in London and made a lot of money there. When Moses Montefiore was a young man he began to travel, travelling all over Europe and the Middle East, and since there weren't many railways when he started his travels, for many of his journeys he used the big comfortable carriage that now stands in the cage behind you. In the course of his journeys he came to Palestine, as this country was called then, and found himself very much shocked and distressed by the condition of his fellow-Jews who lived in Jerusalem. Over the past few centuries more and more of them had been coming – coming back, as they saw it – to Jerusalem, and not only Sephardi Jews from the Mediterranean but Jews from all over Europe: Ashkenazi Jews, from Germany and from Russia and from heaven knows where else, many of them old people wanting at least to die in the holy city of Jerusalem. But there was nowhere to live except inside the city walls: outside there were only the Arab tribesmen and these were, or were believed to be dangerous. So inside the city walls there were crammed not only the Turks, who now owned the whole country, and the Arabs who used to own it and had their Holy Places there, and all kinds of Christians who had *their* Holy Places there, but now more and more Jews who had their Holy Places there too.

'So, when Moses Montefiore first came to Jerusalem, the conditions in the city were really pretty dreadful, and worst of all for the Jews who were usually the poorest and so had to live in the very nastiest of the slums. Moses Montefiore decided that something must be done, and he came to the conclusion that, outside the city walls, it wasn't nearly so dangerous as people supposed; and that there was plenty of room to build there because nobody else did. So he bought from the Turks this land that we're standing on, or rather sitting on, and just below us, facing the walls of Jerusalem, he built a row of pretty little houses with a wide verandah running all along the front to shade them from the sun –'

'Mishkenot Sha'ananim!' interrupted Ezra excitedly.

'Mishkenot Sha'ananim,' agreed William – 'in English, the Peaceful Dwellings, which is the name of the little row of houses where you are staying, and which are now, as you know, guest-houses where the city of Jerusalem offers accommodation to artists and scholars of all kinds from all over the world. But what Moses Montefiore built them for, was to house poor families of Jews. And he did more than just build houses with more room to live in than they had in the slums of the city. He wanted the people who came out here to be able to earn their livings, so he sent to England for all the pieces needed to make a windmill, together with an English workman who knew how to put the pieces together. For he intended the Jews of this place to earn their living by grinding corn. But I'm sorry to say the Jews didn't stay here long. For all that Sir Moses said – it was Queen Victoria who made him a 'Sir' – the Jews felt themselves in danger out here on the hill, and all too soon they went back to the slums of the city. And the little houses and the windmill just fell into decay until –'

All this while, on the other side of the windmill, Ferry had been lying, panting and dizzy, flat on his belly on the stones. At last he began to breathe a bit more slowly and quietly, to get a little, just a little more air into his lungs. Slowly, very slowly, for this was all he could manage, he dragged himself up from the ground till he crouched, shivering, on four torn, bruised paws. Slowly, very slowly, he began to crawl away from the windmill, and down the path that separated it from some rows of little houses just beside it. He didn't know where he was going or why, only that he was alive, and while he was

alive, he must move, must look for – he didn't know what. The wind was getting up now, and it lashed coldly at him as he staggered down the path, and so he turned aside into a cross path, which was sheltered from the wind by the houses on each side of it.

*   *   *

'. . . And the little houses and the windmill just fell into decay,' William was saying, 'until a very few years ago. Then, after Jerusalem belonged to the Jews again, two thousand years after the Romans had turned them out of it, Sir Moses' houses were done up and became Mishkenot Sha'ananim; the windmill was done up and stands here looking like what it is, a handsome English windmill with Sir Moses' carriage safe in a cage beside it; the Music Centre where you are, I know, taking a masterclass later this morning, was built just below us; and on the other side of the path there, you can see that a village of pretty houses is growing up, with no smelly, noisy motor-cars allowed in it. This is the village of Yemin Moshe, which means, roughly, Moses' Place, and almost everyone who lives there is a writer or artist or something of that sort, and I am one of them.'

'How do *you* come to be living here?' asked Ezra. 'You are an Englishman, aren't you?'

- William laughed. 'Whether I'm really living here or not is something my wife and I still aren't sure about,' he said. 'But I certainly am staying here and have been for quite a time, and since you aren't quite due at your class yet and I've still a bit of work to do on you before I let you go, I'll tell you how it happened – that is, if you'll keep on gazing on the city of Jerusalem and not turn round politely to look at me.'

'I promise,' said Ezra obediently, and added, 'And I thank you, William, for making me sit here, for I have never gazed at Jerusalem for so long before, and it lifts my heart to do so. But now tell me why *you* came here.'

William said, 'It was all because of a picture postcard. When I was twelve, my grandparents came on a trip to Jerusalem, and they sent me a postcard of the Golden Gate in Jerusalem's wall, and that postcard changed my life, for this was no ordinary picture postcard. It was a postcard of a painting by David Roberts, a Scottish artist who came here, I suppose, about the time that Moses Montefiore first did. I looked at it and I knew that I wanted to be a painter, and that I wanted to paint in the Holy Land. But I never wanted to paint *places* here, as David Roberts did. For what reason I don't know, I never wanted to paint anything but faces, and, except at art school where I had to do what I was told, faces are all I've ever painted.'

'Were you at art school in England?' Ezra asked, 'and did your parents mind you becoming a painter? I've always been told that the English like their children to take up professions they think of as sensible ones, with good salaries and pensions which, heaven knows, are not available for us artists.'

'Well, my parents are perfectly sensible,' said William cheerfully, 'even though they have a great respect for artists, which is not so rare among the English as you may have been led to believe. We came to an agreement that if I worked hard at school and passed enough examinations to be able to go in for a training for a safer job if anything went wrong with my notion of being a painter, then I could go straight from school to art school, and what I did after art school was up to me. And since my twelve-year old dream still held good, what I did was to come here and paint faces. You may move now. I've almost finished with yours.'

Ezra turned round and stretched himself. 'You don't want me for the oil painting, do you?' he said. 'But when will it be done? When shall I be able to see it?'

'I'll be going back to my studio to work on it straight-away,' William explained, 'and I'll go on with it steadily now while I still have you clear in my mind as well as in the sketches you've so patiently let me make. I'll cer-tainly have the painting finished by Hanukáh, which this year is about two weeks before Christmas. If you'll be in

Israel for Hanukáh, you can come to our Hanukáh party, and I can show it to you then.'

'I should greatly have liked to light the Hanukáh lamps with you,' said Ezra, 'for that is my favourite festival of all the Jewish year, the only one that tells of a time when the Jews fought back against their oppressors. And now the Roman Empire they fought against is long since gone, yet the Jews are still celebrating their struggle against the Romans. But alas, I shan't be in Israel for this year's Hanukáh.'

'Then what about Christmas?' suggested William. 'Come to our Christmas party, and see both your portrait and our boy Jakie's first Christmas tree.'

'I wish I could,' said Ezra smiling, 'but you see, tomorrow I go off for a concert tour in America, and then I play in Paris, and for Christmas I have promised to be back in Switzerland. Only after that shall I be in Israel again.'

'Will you be back for Twelfth Night, which is January 6th?' William tried again.

'Yes, I shall be,' said Ezra, in pleased surprise. 'But Twelfth Night – that is Epiphany, surely, and a Christian festival. I can understand you celebrating Christmas because most people do. But for a Jew to celebrate Epiphany – or – am I wrong? Perhaps you are not a Jew?'

'Well, I'm a kind of Jew,' William said, 'A Jew by inheritance though not by practice. I'm almost ashamed to tell you how lucky my own family has been, when your story is so tragic, but the fact is that I came from one of those families of German Jews who had lived in the same little university town in Germany from time out of mind, as the saying is, always in professions like pub-

lishing or lawyering or simply being scholars. My grandfather was a professor of mathematics in the university
and, I'm told – for, of course, I wasn't born then – the
year before Hitler came to power, my grandfather called
the family together and said that it was time to move on.
He said he was sure that Hitler *would* get power and
would carry out all the threats he'd been making against
the Jews. The family took his advice, and some of the
uncles went off to Sweden where a distant part of our
family was already living and there they all still are. My
grandfather had, it turned out, already got himself invited to one of the London colleges, so to London they all
went, with all their money and their furniture and everything, just in time. My father was only a schoolboy then,
but he was old enough to fight in the last war, and then
he, and my grandparents too, became English. My
mother is a non-Jewish Englishwoman, and so I am
half-Jewish by birth and by feeling, but not at all Jewish
by practice.'

'Apart that is from celebrating Jewish festivals,' com-
mented Ezra. 'Yours is a happy story, and I am always
glad to hear one. But don't you celebrate rather a lot of
festivals?'

William laughed. 'Maybe we do,' he said. 'But Rose
and I have not been married very long and we like
celebrations and they give us a good excuse for inviting
our friends. But we have a special reason for celebrating
Epiphany this year, which is that on January the sixth,
our baby Jakie will be six months old; and what better day
for a six-months' birthday than the one on which the
three kings brought their presents to the infant Jesus? So

please come, and you shall see your portrait and then, if you like it, you will be happy to stay and share what will be just a very little party of good friends. We live in the third alley down from the windmill, and ours is the corner house on the north side of the first cross-alley.'

'I will surely come,' said Ezra, 'and I will bring just a little present for the baby and I shall certainly like my portrait. And now I must go to my class, or I shall keep my pupils waiting.'

*   *   *

Ferry had crawled slowly, and ever more slowly along the north side of the third alley, but now what little energy he had was all but finished. Yet to lie down and collapse in open ground, right out in even a narrow alley, would be so dangerous as to mean that a cat had completely given up hope of living, and for Ferry, this moment had not quite come; though very nearly. He just managed to crawl under a low iron gate, and there he lay, flat on the stones, his whole body and his head flat on the stones, and his eyes all but closed. This was his very worst moment. If no help came to Ferry, the little black cat, he would soon die.

Then, close beside him, he heard a gentle rustling. With immense difficulty, hardly able to do so, he opened his eyes which had seemed as if they would never open to see anything again – and what *did* he see, right by his head, but two feet in sandals, and above them, hanging almost right down to the ground, a robe of brown wool! Dazed and dizzy as he was, Ferry could hardly know that this brown robe, these sandalled feet were different from

the feet and the robes whose kindly memory had been carried in his cat family for five hundred years. Slowly he opened his eyes still wider, lifted his head just a little from the stones, and then he was looking up into the eyes of a beautiful young woman, and she was looking down into the sad blue-green eyes of a nearly hopeless black cat who was staring imploringly up at her.

The beautiful young woman was Rose, the wife of the painter William, and she had just put their baby Jakie out in his pram to take his morning sleep in the clear cold winter air. She looked down at the cat and she seemed to hear William saying, as he so often said, 'You mustn't feed the wild cats, Rose, or soon we'll have them all over the place.' She half-turned to move away, and then looked down again at this cat's pleading eyes, and suddenly, somehow, her heart was stirred with pity and love as it was when she looked on her baby Jakie; though her baby was happy and strong, and had everything in the world a baby could want and need, and this young cat, she could see, was sad and weak and had nothing at all in the whole wide world. 'Wait a minute, little cat,' she said – it was the first time anyone had ever spoken to him – and she went quickly into her house.

The little cat was too weak to do anything *but* wait. But even if he could have moved, he didn't want to. Somehow he knew, in his cat mind, that the old memory about the goodness of brown robes and sandalled feet was a trustworthy story, even when the feet were small and delicate and the brown robe a fashionable kaftan made not of coarse thick cloth but of fine wool.

Rose came back with a saucer of milk. She put it down on the paving stone by the cat's head, and waited.

The little cat had never tasted milk since he was a tiny kitten. But no cat ever forgets the smell of milk, and this smell was perhaps the only one that could have got the little cat up on to his knees – he hadn't yet the strength to stand up on his four paws – with his mouth splashing down into the milk.

He had never lapped milk from a saucer before, but he put out his rough pink tongue and feebly his tongue took a sip of the milk, a sip of thankful liquid to a dry, parched, thirsty throat. The cat took another sip and another and another. Slowly at first, then faster and faster the little black cat lapped the saucer of milk until every drop was gone. And when the last drop of milk was gone, he had gathered just enough strength to stand up on his four paws and give himself, but still very feebly, the kind of stretch that healthy cats do usually give themselves when they have just finished a meal.

Rose was so glad to see that this poor little cat could get to its feet again that tears of happiness came into her eyes. 'There's a good puss,' she said. 'Oh, what a good puss!' and she said it softly so as not to waken the baby, but not so softly that she wasn't heard by William who was just back from the windmill and coming in at the gate. 'Rose, I've told you,' he said, 'and if I've told you once I've told you a hundred times, you must not feed the wild cats, or we'll have them all over the place.' But he didn't say it angrily, and he put his painting things down on the ground, then came and stood beside her. They put their arms round each other and stood there beside their baby in his pram, both of them looking down at the little black cat who looked up at them with its aquamarine eyes already a little bit brighter for the saucer of milk. William said consideringly, 'He's got interesting eyes, that shabby little cat.'

The cat's eyes flicked quickly, flicked from William and Rose to the baby's pram beside them. Suddenly, and heaven only knows how he found the strength to do it, the cat had leapt up from the paving stones, up on to the pram.

Rose gave a little scream. She thought the cat was going to attack her baby, and was about to rush forward when William caught hold of her arm. 'Wait!' he said. His eyes were quicker than hers and he saw what had happened. The cat had seen a mouse running over the pram cover, running towards the baby's face. Before it could get there, the cat had caught the mouse.

Of course the cat hadn't known he was saving a baby from having a mouse run over its face. All the cat knew was that he, who hadn't eaten for days, had just seen a mouse that no other cat was after; and the milk he had drunk had given him just enough strength to leap on to the pram and to catch the mouse.

So he caught the mouse and he killed it straightaway, never in his life having had the elbow-room to play with a mouse before he killed it, as safe, well-fed cats will usually do. But before he gobbled it down he stood as he always did, hesitating, for a moment, the dead mouse held in his teeth.

He looked to right and to left but there was no other cat to snatch it from him. He was just going to lay the mouse down and tear it to pieces on the pretty blue pram cover that Rose had knitted with her own hands – when something stopped him. It was something that went with the once-useless politeness his mother had taught him, which had so often stopped him from getting his fair share of food on the hill. It was something, perhaps, to do with those age-old memories of comfort from people in sandals and brown robes, and it might have been something he had seen when he looked up into William's eyes. Whatever it was, it held the cat back from eating the much-needed mouse in almost one single mouthful. Instead he jumped off the pram with the mouse still in his mouth, and then laid it down on the pavement at Willaim and Rose's feet.

'*Good* cat!' said Rose, the right response coming automatically to her lips. She turned and cried, 'William, the poor little beast thinks he belongs to us! He's bringing his catch to his owners, like good cats do!'

William looked at the mouse and he looked at the cat. 'Good cat!' he said too, warmly and politely, and then to Rose, 'I think this really is a very good cat. There can't be many cats as starved as he is who'd remember their manners like that, and heaven knows where he learnt them, for he clearly doesn't belong to anyone. I think he's right in supposing he might belong to us, and if you agree, we'll keep him and feed him up; and he'll see that no mice run over Jakie or into the house and this shall be his home. And I think,' he said consideringly, 'I'll do some drawings of him. I like his face.'

'The drawings,' said Rose, 'are your business, but the rest of what you've said I heartily agree with. A cat is just what this home needs, and I can see that this is a young cat who will soon learn our ways if we treat him rightly.'

'What he needs most at the moment,' said William, 'is food and sleep. In fact, since he's already had some milk, I think the best thing for him would be a good long sleep and you can get a dish of food ready for him when he wakes.'

'I'll do that,' said Rose, and William bent down and picked up the little cat who was still crouching there beside his mouse, looking hopefully, pleadingly up at them. The cat had never been picked up before, never even been touched by a human hand and he shivered with terror. But William held him tightly and tickled him behind one ear, an absolutely new feeling for this cat but a good feeling, a safe feeling, a reassuring one, and when William gently laid him down on the goatswool rug in front of the open wood fire, the cat fell immediately asleep, the first safe sleep he had ever known in his life since his mother had turned him off to fend for himself.

William went into the kitchen where Rose was shredding up some pieces left from the chicken that she'd boiled for their supper the night before. 'This will be a very good-looking cat when he's filled out a bit,' he said. 'Certainly I've never seen such beautiful aquamarine eyes on any cat before.'

'What shall we call him?' asked Rose, putting the pieces of chicken into a little saucepan together with a drop of chicken stock: then, half to herself, 'It's such a cold day, his first meal here might as well be a warm one, whatever his name is.'

'We'll call him Ferry,' said William, without needing even a second to think about it. 'Ferry short for feral cat, because a feral cat is what our Ferry is.'

'Ferry – Ferry,' repeated Rose, trying it out. 'Yes, I think that Ferry sounds like just the right name for our cat – but why short for feral cat? What *is* a feral cat?'

'A feral cat,' William explained, 'is a cat, or one of a family of cats, who once used to be domestic in a human home and then took to being wild. You can have feral dogs, too, of course, and even feral plants.'

Rose laughed. 'I don't see how a domestic plant can go wild,' she said. 'You surely don't mean that it picks up its roots and walks out of its garden.'

'The plant doesn't run away,' William told her, 'but its seeds may do. A tree or a flower you plant carefully in your garden can be growing wild all over the country in just a few years if the wind or the birds carry the seeds away from the garden and then let them fall on the ground outside. And I expect that something like that happened to our Ferry. Way back, maybe even hundreds of years back, one of his ancestors was turned out of his home, or maybe even chose to go wild – quite a few cats do seem to prefer to live wild.'

'Not Ferry,' said Rose, washing the knife she'd shredded the chicken with. 'You can see he comes of a good domestic stock, with those nice manners of his, and wanting to guard the baby too. All he wants is a good home with a loving family, like ours. And since it isn't my shopping day, I suggest, William, that before you go off to your studio, you make a trip to the supermarket and buy a tin of cat food and some flea powder, for Ferry is certainly not going to have chicken every day, and he's not going to save our Jakie from mice only to cover him with fleas.'

'Good idea,' said William, warmly, 'and I'll drop in next door, too, and find out what vet they use, so that we can arrange for Ferry to have 'flu injections when he's a bit stronger.' He kissed Rose goodbye, then added as he took a shopping-bag off the hook on the back door, 'I wish we could know just where our own little feral cat has come from.'

'We never shall,' said Rose. She put the chicken-meat in its saucepan on to a wire mat over a very low gas, and then went back to the living room.

*　　*　　*

Since Rose had been a little girl, she had had the habit of telling stories. She told them to her parents and she told them to her dolls, and then she told them to her school-friends. She was no good at making up stories of her own, so she would sometimes tell stories she had heard or read, like fairy stories and ghost stories and stories of adventures; and sometimes she would tell stories about herself and her family.

These days she was looking forward to the time when she could tell stories to Jakie, and to the sister she meant him to have in a year or so, and quite often as she sat alone knitting or sewing she would practise these stories, running them through in her head. This morning, she had done all her housework early while William was up at the windmill with Ezra, and it wasn't her day for shopping. So, while Jakie slept in his pram outdoors and the new cat Ferry by the fire, Rose picked up her knitting, which was a thick winter scarf for William, and decided she would run through one of her stories to the sleeping cat. And because he had only just come into the family and knew nothing about it, she decided to tell him, in her soft gentle voice, the story of how she came to be living in the artists' village beside Jerusalem:

'My great-grandfather,' she began, 'which is to say, my father's father's father, was a tailor in a small town in Russia, and, by all accounts, a cheerful, lively go-ahead man who married a good, cheerful, hard-working wife. But the town they lived in wasn't big enough for even a good tailor to make much of a living there. They wondered whether it mightn't be better to move to a bigger town, but it wasn't easy for Jews to move around in

Russia just as they wanted to, and anyway, as my great-grandfather said, in a bigger town there might well be enough tailors already. So what with one thing and another, they decided to leave Russia altogether and sail away to America where, they'd heard, the Jews were just as well treated as anybody else, and had been ever since they had first started going to America in the sailing ships; and there, it was said, any hard-working man could make a good living.

'But about eighty years ago, when my great-grandfather and great-grandmother first came to America, it wasn't so easy as all that. There were a lot of new people just come to New York, the town where they settled, new Jews, and new Irish and new Germans and Italians and I don't know who else, and for a long time

after they first landed, most of these new people were very poor. At first my great-grandfather did odd jobs for any other tailor who would employ him, and my great-grandmother, who had just started having children of her own, would make a little money by looking after the children of other women who had to go out to work.

'However,' said Rose, 'Great-grandfather was not only a hard worker, he was also a very good tailor, and before too long he got a regular job working for a man with a big tailor's shop, and by the time their last baby was born, my great-grandparents were able to move out of the crowded slums of New York City and to rent a nice little house up in Brooklyn, which is a pleasant airy part of New York where a lot of Jews still like to live.

'Great-grandfather's eldest son Jacob – it's his name that we gave to Jakie,' she explained to the sleeping cat, 'Grandfather Jacob became a tailor too, and he started off in the big shop where his father was still working, but what *he* wanted to do was to set up on his own, and soon he was able to do so, what with the money he'd saved from his wages and a bit more his father was able to give him. What *he* did was to set up an establishment, not exactly a shop, in a very expensive part of the city, where he made very expensive, very good clothes, for very rich men. And he married a very nice girl from Brooklyn – that's my Grandmother Rachel, and she still lives there in the big house he bought for her, for he made rather a lot of money.

'Grandfather Jacob's eldest son was called Stanley, and *he* was *my* father, and he too decided to become a tailor. But he didn't want to make good expensive clothes for just a few rich men, but good cheap clothes for many, many more men who paid much less money. First he opened one shop over in West Side New York, and then another and another and another, all in different places but never where rich people lived, and he found, as he expected, that the poorer people were as ready as the rich to recognise good quality and value for money. So my father made lots and lots of money and he married my mother Chaya, whose father was an important jeweller. My mother was very pretty – well, I think she still *is* very pretty – and they still live in New York in a big apartment with a view right over Central Park.

'I was the baby of the family,' Rose told the cat, 'and by the time I was born my eldest brother Melvyn had already gone into the tailoring business, and my eldest sister Loretta was thinking of getting married. Even my next sister Marilyn was ten years older than me, so I was a bit lonely, which is, I expect, why I started telling stories. But I was pretty happy most of the time until I was about fourteen and then, I don't know why, I got discontented with the kind of life my parents wanted me to have, just having a good time and growing up and then getting married to some nice Jewish boy, like my mother had done and my grandmother and my great-grandmother and then having just the same kind of life as theirs. I wanted something different.

'Actually, I do know what it was that made me discon-tented, and this was that lots of the older kids in our group, and some of the brothers and sisters of my friends, they weren't just going on in the same old ways but getting out and seeing the world, even if most of them did come back in the end and marry a nice Jewish boy or girl and settle down as their parents had done. And because the State of Israel had been made just a few years before, the first Jewish State since before the Romans, lots of these Jewish kids from America went out to Israel and worked on the *Kibbutzim* there. So I went on and on at my parents till they let me do the same, and three years ago, when I was eighteen, they let me come out to join a Kibbutz not far from Bethesda.

'I'll tell you what a kibbutz is,' Rose said to Ferry, 'because I wouldn't expect a town cat like you to know. It's a farm where everything belongs to everybody and nobody has anything of their own, and everybody shares all the work and, except for sleeping, they spend all their lives together, eating and amusing themselves together as well as working together. Of course, not all kibbutzim are quite the same, but on the kibbutz I joined, even the children almost belonged to everybody, all living together in a special children's house, with their parents coming to visit them.

'I have to tell you frankly, Ferry, that I pretty soon decided that kibbutz life was not for me, at least, not for ever. Of course it's fun when you're young, being with a lot of other young people, all working together for something you believe in, and the evenings were great fun, singing and dancing together, and I liked some of the work, especially when it was my turn to help with the children. But I soon knew I'd hate to spend all my life with a lot of other people around all the time, and I simply wouldn't stand for other people looking after my children and bringing them up. I could see it was a way of life that lots of people loved, even when they were quite old. But I knew it wasn't for me.

'So I was wondering what I should do next, whether to go back to New York, which I didn't feel ready to do yet, or maybe go up to Jerusalem and get me a job, like in a craft shop or something. And I was leaning over a gate one evening, at sunset time after the work was done, when I saw William come tramping down the path towards me. He was walking around Israel looking for faces to paint, and when he came to our kibbutz the first face he saw there was mine. He fell in love with me and I fell in love with him and we got married almost right away, and luckily William was getting well known for his work, so we could buy this house we're living in now, though I don't know how long we'll live here. Because though William and I intend to live pretty well happy ever after, and I expect we shall, there's just one thing we do nearly quarrel about, and that's whether we shall, in the end, go and live in England to be near William's parents or in America to be near mine.

'I'll just tell you one odd thing to finish up with,' Rose said to Ferry, who stirred as she spoke, 'and you ought to be very flattered by it: William wanted to draw your face as soon as he saw you. Yet though he fell in love with me, he never even thought of painting me till nearly six months ago, when Jakie was born.'

While Rose had been telling her story, Ferry had been sleeping, sleeping longer and more deeply than he had ever slept before. He had been sleeping to make up for the long hard months on the hillside where no cat ever dares to sleep sound, must never do more than catnap, ready to wake in an instant to meet danger. He was sleeping away his terrified, terrifying escape from the dogs, down the hill, over across the roaring traffic, with racing paws still sore and torn from the rough ground. He was sleeping safely, for the first time, in his own home.

As Rose was finishing her story, Ferry started to wake up, with the sound of her voice like a gentle purring in his ears. And as he began to wake, it was to a smell the like of which he had never smelt before, except in the faintest of wafts, from far away. It was the smell of clean, fresh, cooked food, and it came, this fine smell, not from over the walls of Jerusalem, but from near, from very near at hand. Ferry opened his eyes and staggered with difficulty to his feet. He stretched his aching legs, then looked around, and there, standing beside him, were the sandals and the long brown robe of the young woman who had given him the milk that had saved his life.

'So you've woken up at last,' said Rose to Ferry. 'Well, it's just about time I got Jakie up for his lunch, but I'll give you yours first. Come along, now,' and she went into the kitchen where she turned the chicken out of the saucepan on to a pretty blue willow-pattern saucer.

'There's just two of those left,' she said to him, 'so you can have this one for your meat and the other one with the chip in it for your milk, and then you'll have your own sets of china, just like Jakie and us.'

She put the still steaming saucer on to a piece of newspaper she laid on the floor near the back door, and then she tapped the saucer with her fingernail. Ferry somehow understood straightaway what she meant.

Stiff-legged and brave he walked, though very cautiously at first, over to the blue saucer, to the first meal
that had ever been specially prepared for him. He sniffed
it, he made a dart at it with his paw and then, more
daringly, with his paw he hooked out a piece of the warm
meat on to the newspaper, and then he swallowed it in a
gulp.

'You seem to have got the idea,' said Rose, 'so I'll just
slip out and fetch Jakie,' and by the time she had opened
the door, Ferry was so absorbed in his meal that he didn't
even lift his head from the meat.

William was coming back with the cat food and the flea
powder as Rose was lifting Jakie out of the pram, and
they all came into the house together. The food was
cooler now and Ferry was gobbling it up straight from the
saucer. He just lifted his head for a moment as they came
in and settled down to his eating again, as Rose handed
the baby to his father and began heating up his lunchtime
bottle. She was taking it out of the warm water when
Ferry, who had licked his saucer clean, began to scratch
at the back door, stopping now and then to look up
hopefully at William.

'Does he want to run away?' asked Rose, shocked at
the thought.

'William answered. 'No – not for a minute. He's a
well-bred cat and he wants to be a clean cat, that's all – I
must make a cat door for him.'

He opened the back door and left it ajar, and Ferry
walked out into the garden and in a few moments, to
Rose's intense relief, he walked in again, straight back to
the rug by the fire and there he lay down. Rose took the

baby and the bottle and went upstairs to change the baby's nappy before she fed him, but William came in to the living room and bent down to the rug. Ferry, lying there, again felt a human hand on him, a hand scratching his head, a finger tickling his ear, and, from Ferry's throat there came a rough rusty voice he had never heard himself make before, a rough rusty noise that soon settled down into a smooth steady roar, the noise of a safe, happy cat in its own home, purring.

*   *   *

The next day Ferry washed himself all over for the first time in his life, but though he looked a bit less raggedy as a result, he was still a long way from appearing a well-groomed healthy cat. Too much of his fur was still rough and rusty instead of a smooth plushy black, and it didn't cover nearly enough flesh on his bones. But from then onwards he washed himself all over at least once every day, and every day it was a healthier, handsomer cat that he washed.

At the end of Ferry's first week in William and Rose's house, the baby Jakie, who was lying on the rug beside the fire, turned himself over for the first time from his tummy on to his back. He had caught sight of Ferry and wanted to touch him, and when he had rolled over he could touch the cat and he chortled with joy. It was one of Ferry's hind legs that Jakie had got hold of, and Rose, watching anxiously, saw that Ferry didn't put his claws out in self-defence; and when Jakie let go, Ferry didn't run away, but patted the baby's hand with his front paw, as if to say, 'Let's go on playing.' Soon the baby and the cat did play with each other, both of them understanding, it seemed, that though they could hurt each other, they must not; and if one hurt the other accidentally, the one who was hurt seemed always to realise it was an accident, and never hurt back.

Once Rose was assured that the cat would never hurt the baby, she was always happy for Ferry to take his morning naps on Jakie's pram, which he liked to do whenever the weather was warm enough, that harsh winter, for the baby to be put out in the garden. 'There always might be another mouse on the pram,' Rose explained to William, and, though there never was, Rose felt that Jakie was safer with Ferry on guard.

When Ferry had been with the family for just two weeks, he climbed on to Rose's lap as she sat on the sofa, finishing off William's scarf, and stood up on her lap and rubbed his forehead against hers, which is a cat's way of kissing. 'Let's see if he loves me too,' said William, pulling Ferry on to his own lap, and Ferry did just the same thing to him. 'I think,' said William to Ferry, 'you are ready to sit for your portrait now,' and when Ferry had climbed down back to the rug to sleep, William started on the first of what were to be a famous series of drawings of his family cat.

By the time that Ferry had been living in his own home for a month, he was a fine sleek handsome black cat with bright blue-green eyes that shone like aquamarines. He had his own cat door now, and he was beginning to venture out of his own garden and make the acquaintance of the other domestic cats who lived in the street. In the pack on the hillside there had never been more than a grudging acceptance of each other. Among the house-cats in the narrow street in Moses' Place there was more; almost all of them were friends.

Opposite Ferry's house lived two smooth grey brothers, Bartie and Andrew, and their passion was for jumping. Fortunately their sculptor-owners had a big studio full of big sculptures tough enough not to be hurt by cats jumping from one piece to another. Even when they went out into the street Bartie and Andrew liked to jump from their own wall over to Ferry's wall and back, and he, though he never jumped back with them, would rub noses when they arrived. Then in the next house to Ferry lived the sleepy black green-eyed Persian, Treacle, and sometimes when she lay out in her garden in a patch of sun, Ferry would jump down into it and snuggle up beside her. He was on nose-rubbing terms with the tabby mother and daughter, Grace and Eliza, who lived with the professor down the street, great hunters the pair of them, who often passed Ferry's gate on their way to the wilder hunting-grounds beyond. Neither he nor any of the other cats took to Pinky with the sandy-coloured long hair, for she was much too smarmy, too ready to arch her back and rub against anyone's legs: her mistress, who painted bad religious pictures to sell to those modern pilgrims, the tourists, was just the same in a human way, but, luckily for them, neither realised how soppy they were, and they believed themselves the most popular characters in the street. But most important of all, Ferry was approved of by the Abyssinian cat with the tufted ears, Sam Khan, who lived with a writer in the middle house on the north side and was the unquestioned lord of the manor. Down the street Sam Khan would stroll, dropping in through every cat door but Pinky's, and the other cats would welcome him and even stand aside while he took a bite or a sip from their saucers. It was a proud day for Ferry when Sam Khan discovered his new cat door and came in.

None of the other domestic cats chose to come into each other's houses: apart from Sam Khan, they met in the street or, occasionally, in each other's gardens, as Ferry and Treacle did. Against the half-wild cats of this side of the hill, all the domestic cats guarded their doors most jealously, and none more so than Ferry. Once he was established as a house-cat, it was as if he had become so terrified of any memory of the old harsh life that he was even fiercer than the other domestic cats when guarding his door against intruders.

Certainly the old life had left its marks on Ferry, and once outside his own gate he was by far the most timid of the house-cat colony. He would never walk so far from his home that he couldn't see it if he looked back, and he was always terrified by dogs, even of the friendly old pug dog Mimi two doors down whom the other cats treated as a kind of honorary cat. When a strange dog appeared, the other cats would, of course, frush up their tails and arch their backs till every hair stood on end, and then, furiously, hiss. Not Ferry. No sooner did a dog come in sight than Ferry was over the nearest wall or under the nearest gate, and the neighbours, when they saw him arrive, would say, 'Ferry must have met a dog again.'

Another mark left by the old life was Ferry's absolute refusal, now, to eat anything he caught. With so many cats, domestic and wild, prowling around the artists' colony, there never was, in fact, very much to catch. Ferry like a good working cat, kept his own house and garden free of mice, and snapped at any lizard that came his way, but never did he eat his catch. He always brought it as a present to William or to Rose, who would always say politely something like, 'Thank you, Ferry,' or 'Clever Ferry,' before they threw it away.

*   *   *

The Jews still lived by the ancient calendar that had been worked out in the days before it was discovered that the earth went round the sun and not the other way round.

So though, for Jews, the Jewish Holy Days went on happening just as they always had happened, by the Western calendar they moved about very considerably. It so fell out that the year of Ferry's discovery of his family was one when the Jewish festival of Hanukáh fell so close to Christmas that William and Rose decided that they wouldn't have a Hanukáh party of their own. Instead they accepted an invitation from Sam Khan's master and mistress who, of course, invited them to take Jakie along in his Moses basket. When Christmas Day came, William and Rose asked Sam Khan's master and mistress over for Christmas lunch, and, naturally, Sam Khan dropped in too.

But this Christmas, which was both Jakie and Ferry's first, proved a sad disappointment so far as the cat was concerned. Most of the time he had been living on tinned cat food and scraps with an occasional bit of fish for a treat, and on this diet he had thrived. But for a Christmas surprise for him, Rose had the idea of buying him a chicken liver and frying it up in the best olive oil. Not surprisingly this dish proved much too rich for Ferry's still delicate stomach. He took just a few mouthfuls and then he sicked it all up again – 'Lucky it was on the kitchen floor and not on the living-room rug,' said William cheerfully, mopping up the mess – and Sam Khan, who had just arrived, licked the saucer clean and looked all the better for it.

By the time it came to Twelfth Night, however, every-thing was promising well. Everybody whom William and Rose had invited would be able to come. Baby Jakie woke up in an especially cheerful mood, as if he knew it was his six-month birthday, and William and Rose decided, then and there, that January the sixth should count as Ferry's first birthday since they guessed him to be just about a year old (and they weren't far out). Moreover, when the postman came that morning, he brought the parcels that should have arrived from the grandparents long since, from the American grandparents in time for Hanukáh, from the English grandparents in time for Christmas. Naturally both sets of grandparents had been told of Ferry's arrival, and to everyone's delight there were, among the splendid presents in the parcels, presents for him too. Rose's parents had sent from America a blue velvet collar with a brass dingle-dangle on it, and on the dingle-dangle was engraved his name FERRY with his address and telephone number in case he ever got lost, though with Ferry sticking so close to home, this wasn't likely. William's parents, from England, had sent an outsize tortoiseshell toothbrush.

It might as well be said here and now that both presents were enormously successful. Ferry took to his collar straightaway and showed it off to the other cats with evident pride, the first cat collar in that street, though soon all the other cats had collars too, except for Bartie and Andrew, whose owners felt that collars might be dangerous for such athletic leapers. As for the toothbrush, Ferry quickly learned to jump every evening into William's or Rose's lap and be thoroughly brushed, all down the spine, first the wrong way of the fur then the right way, gently over the tummy and tail, and best of all, the top of the head and the whiskers. And with constant

brushing, Ferry's already beautiful black coat grew glossier and more lustrous than ever.

As a first-birthday present from Ferry's own family, Rose had begged some fresh catmint from a friend who was the Director of the Jerusalem Botanic Gardens; she cut some grey felt into a mouselike shape and stuffed it with the fresh herb, and there was a catnip mouse, which Ferry was enraptured by, as almost all cats always are. The smell of it drove him wild with delight and for a couple of days he was forever picking it up with his teeth or claws, throwing it into the air and catching it, and then laying it down and growling at it. In the end he tore it quite to pieces, threw the bits of felt and catmint all over the floor, then strolled out of his door to take a rest with Treacle, and never thought of that mouse again; which was, as William and Rose both knew, the way of cats with catnip mice.

* * *

As he had been asked to, Ezra came early that evening. William took him straight into the studio to see his portrait. It was indeed superb; when it was publicly shown, critics were to say it was the best portrait William had yet done. Ezra looked at it and all he said when he was in the studio was, 'You can see that I was holding my flute and looking at Jerusalem when you painted it,' and with that, William was more than satisfied. Then, as they left the studio, Ezra added with a grin, 'You can even see in my face that I was sitting by a windmill with a carriage in a cage behind me,' and both men laughed.

They went into the living-room, and Ezra greeted Rose

and handed her the basket he was carrying, a rush basket with a lid, and inside it seven parcels all in the same pretty paper but all of different sizes. 'These are for your baby son,' said Ezra. 'The biggest to be opened today, so please will you open it for him now?' This Rose excitedly did, and inside the parcel was a carved wooden bear, just about as big as Jakie's head.

'This bear is from the city of Berne which is named for bears,' said Ezra. 'The bears are made of clean carved wood so they are safe for a baby to suck and they won't easily break. Next Epiphany you will please open the second largest parcel which has the second largest bear in it, and the next year when it is the turn of the next largest, the little boy will be able to open his parcel for himself; and he will soon discover that some of the bears are out for a walk, as this one is, and some of them are sitting down and taking a rest, as bears very often do. So every year, please, give him an Epiphany bear until by the eighth year, when he opens the smallest parcel and finds the smallest bear of all, he himself will be too big to think of putting it in his mouth; and he will have a family of seven bears, from one as big as his thumbnail for when

he is seven and a half years old down to this one which is as big as his head.'

William took the bear from Rose and rolled it about in his hands, trying to imagine how it would feel to the small fumbling hands of Jakie. He said formally to Ezra, 'You will have given our son much pleasure for many years to come. Thank you.' He put the bear on the table by the sofa and every so often during the evening he picked it up and rolled it in his hands. Each time he did so Ezra smiled, seeing he had brought a present that would give as much pleasure to the father now as to the baby in the years to come.

Rose said, 'I'll take the basket upstairs and put it safely away in my treasure chest,' which was an old brass chest from India that stood at the foot of their bed. She was coming down the stairs again when there was a knock at the front door, and she opened it to find on the doorstep one of the other two guests of the evening.

This was Brother Felix, a Franciscan friar who had come to Jerusalem from Germany. No sooner did he walk into the living-room in his brown robe and sandal-led feet than Ferry jumped up from the rug by the fire and ran to Brother Felix and rubbed his head against Brother Felix's legs, purring loudly.

'That's extraordinary!' exclaimed William. 'Ferry's usually most standoffish with strangers, but it's as if he knew you. Do you know him?'

'I wish I did,' said Brother Felix, 'but I am quite certain that I have never met him before. Clearly this is a sagacious cat who knows that our Franciscan Order has a special care for animals, and therefore a cat who has a great liking and respect for our Franciscan Order.

Rose laughed. 'Not a bit of it,' she said. 'What our Ferry likes, as I soon discovered, is brown robes and sandals. I was wearing my brown wool kaftan and sandals when I first met him, and whenever I put these things on, Ferry is always especially loving and friendly.'

'Ah, but maybe that is because one of his ancestors knew and loved a Franciscan,' said Brother Felix. Rose and William laughed, but Ezra said seriously, 'That could well have been. I think that is very possible.'

At that moment another knock on the door announced the last guest of the evening, all of the guests being people whom William had met because he had painted their faces and who had since become family friends. This last arrival was Dr Nora, an Arab woman who had come from the town of Tangiers in Morocco to help look after the children in hospital in Jerusalem. Ferry was still standing by Brother Felix, and no sooner had Dr Nora been introduced to Ezra, the only one there except Ferry whom she didn't know, than she said, 'Where did you get that handsome cat? He is exactly like the cats we have in my father's home in Morocco.'

'That's our Ferry,' said William, as they all sat down. 'He just walked, or rather, crawled into our garden one day, and a miserable little starveling he was then. But where he came from, we haven't the faintest idea.'

'May I take him for a minute?' asked Dr Nora. She lifted Ferry on to her lap and scratched his head so that he would know she was a person who understood cats. Then she lifted his chin and exclaimed, 'But this is extraordinary!'

'What is?' they all asked. Dr Nora said in an excited voice, 'This is! Look here! Do you see, right under his chin, three coarse white hairs?'

They each had a look, and yes, it was so, right under Ferry's chin, hidden away so that you could see them only if you lifted his chin as Dr Nora had done, there were three coarse white hairs among the black velvet fur.

'He *must* come from the same family as our home cats,' said Dr Nora, 'for all the jet-black cats among them have those three white hairs, and have done for generations. And never have I known or heard of any other cats that did.'

'Then I wonder how this one got to Jerusalem,' said Brother Felix.

'How he came to Jerusalem I can't say,' said Dr Nora. 'But how he, or, rather, his family could have come to this country is easy to guess. There are two distinct sides to my own family. Half of us are doctors, which is the side that I come from, and half of us are merchants. For hundreds of years now my cousins have been trading all around the Mediterranean Sea, and what is more likely than that one of my cousins took one of our house-cats on to his ship to keep down the rats and the mice?

'What's more, for some time the trading cousins had, I know, a house in Jaffa, so such a ship's cat, or such a ship's cat's kitten, might well have been taken ashore to live there. So,' she ended, 'I can well see how one of our cats might have got to Jaffa, but it's much harder to guess how one of our cats might have come all the way from there up to Jerusalem.'

'Let me have a guess then,' said Brother Felix. 'Perhaps

it happened, maybe hundreds of years ago, that one of our brothers who was coming up to Jerusalem from Jaffa, was given a kitten by one of your cousins. And if that kitten was a female, it would explain how – what's his name? – how Ferry's ancestors arrived here.'

'This would make sense,' agreed Ezra. 'For, unless we believe that all of us, cats and humans alike, learn from our parents' experience, how could any of us poor creatures survive? And if one of this cat's ancestors was cared for by a Franciscan brother, this could explain why he turns with such love and trust to people in long brown robes and sandals.'

'So now we know,' said Rose, 'What William once said we never could know, which is where our Ferry came from.'

'Oh no you don't,' said Dr Nora solemnly. 'You only know, or rather, you've only guessed, a part of the story. What you don't know is how Ferry's great-great – I don't know how many times-great – grandmother came to be in Morocco in the first place.'

'Do *you* know that?' everyone else asked, more or less at the same time.

'As a matter of fact, I do,' said Dr Nora, 'and if you want, I will tell you the story.'

'Oh yes,' said Rose enthusiastically. She loved being told stories as much as she liked telling them, and this time it was clear that everyone else wanted the story too, so Dr Nora began:

*　　*　　*

'This story has been told in my family for well over five hundred years,' she said. 'Every eldest son has told it to his children in just the same room in just the same house, and when the other sons, and the daughters went to homes of their own, they told the story to their children there. I don't expect the telling of it has changed much in all those five hundred years.

'It begins round about the year thirteen-hundred-and-seventy as the Christians count the years, when the London ship *Unicorn* put in at Tangiers, which is one of the chief ports of Morocco, and the home of my family, then as it is now. The ship *Unicorn* under its master Captain Fitzwarren came from London to Tangiers almost every year, bringing goods from the North to trade for goods from the South. He would bring wool from Yorkshire and furs from the Baltic and dried salt cod from Norway and sometimes, from the far far North, a precious yellow stone called amber which was thought in Morocco to bring great good fortune, because its properties are almost magical –'

'Yes, they are,' said Rose dreamily, hardly breaking the story. 'My grandmother has an amber necklace, and if you rub the beads till they are warm, they will pick up little pieces of paper –'

'– And scraps of silk, too,' agreed Dr Nora, 'and amber is still believed to be especially valuable as an amulet to preserve the wearer from harm, so it is always in great demand with us. Then from Morocco Captain Fitz-warren would take back to the North almonds and brassware and carpets and spices, and still rarer goods that came in from the heart of Africa, with the camel caravans from over the Sahara desert.

'My great-great – let's just say my ancestor – my ancestor then was a doctor. In those days, the Arab doctors of the Mediterranean knew much more of the art of medicine than the doctors of Europe did. So when, on one of his visits to Tangiers, Captain Fitzwarren fell ill, he had no hesitation about asking for the best doctor in town, and he was sent to my ancestor who cured him. Ever after, each time the *Unicorn* came into Tangiers, Captain Fitzwarren would pay a courtesy call on my ancestor, and bring him a present from the North.

'This time, the time of my story, when the doorkeeper let Captain Fitzwarren into our house, my ancestor found that the Captain had a boy with him, an English boy about fifteen years old, who carried a covered basket.

'"Greetings, my friend," said the Captain to the doctor. "I have brought you a new kind of present this time and one that I hope will give pleasure to you and your family. In this basket that my cabin-boy here is carrying, there are ten gallipots of the best honey from the wild land of Scotland. I bought it in Aberdeen harbour when I was on my way to Norroway to collect a cargo of pine trees for ships' masts. It's the taste of the summer heather the bees feed on that gives this honey its special flavour, the best, they say, in all the North."

'"I thank you warmly, Master Fitzwarren," said my ancestor. "Indeed, we in Tangiers badly need a bit of something sweet to cheer our lives which are bitter and sorrowful now and likely to get worse."

'"Why, what's the matter?" Captain Fitzwarren asked, and my ancestor explained that the year before,

just after the *Unicorn* had left for England, a dreadful plague had attacked the cats of Morocco and nearly all of them had died.

'I expect it was what we call the cat 'flu,' said Dr Nora, 'and since we've only just learnt how to prevent it, it's not surprising that in those days even the Arab doctors had no idea what to do. Because of this dreadful cat plague, my ancestor told Captain Fitzwarren, there was hardly a cat still alive in Tangiers, and so the city was over-run with rats and mice. And he and all the other doctors of the city were desperately worried, for they knew, long before the doctors of Europe knew it, that where you were over-run with rats and mice, you were likely to have bad human disease and probably the plague, which was then the worst human disease of all, and not even the Arab doctors knew how to cure it. "So grateful as I am for the honey you have brought me," my ancestor finished, "what we need most in Tangiers at the moment is cats – good professional cats. The cat disease is over, but there's hardly a skilled working cat left in the city. A good ratter and mouser is, at the moment, worth its weight in gold."

'The captain slapped his knee. "My goodness gracious me!" he exclaimed, and he turned to his boy. "Now's your chance, my lad!" he said. "You empty out that basket and go back to the ship and put your Bessy in the basket and bring her along. What the doctor here will pay you for her will set you up with a bit of money to start trading with, and then you'll be well on the way to making your fortune at last."

' "But not by selling Bessy!" cried the boy. "I could

never, never sell Bessy – she's all I've got in the world."

' "Tush, boy," said the Captain impatiently. "She's only a cat, when all's said and done! You've got to look out for yourself in this world, but since you don't seem to know how to, then I'll do it for you. You go back to the *Unicorn*, and you put your Bessy into this basket and bring her back here double-quick, and that's an ORDER!"

'The boy didn't dare to protest any more. He emptied out the pots of honey and ran off with the basket, and while he was gone the Captain explained that this was a country boy who'd come to London port and offered himself as a cabin-boy, begging that his cat should be allowed to sail with him.

' "And being a kind-hearted man, and seeing as how there's always rats and mice aboard a ship and more on mine than our ship's cat Tibbs could cope with, I agreed", said the Captain, "and I will say for that Bessy that she's the best ratter and mouser I ever did come across in all my born days, just as that lad is the best cabin-boy I ever did come across in all my born days, and right sorry I am to order him to part with his good beast. But business is business, and since it's the lad's intention to make his fortune, as he's forever telling me, he might as well start when he's given a chance that's not likely ever to come again, for heaven knows he's got nothing else in the world to trade with, nothing but his cat in all the world –"

'At that moment the boy came back with tears rolling down his cheeks. He clearly had his cat Bessy in the basket, for from it came a continuous, desolate noise of a cat crying and wailing and lamenting. "The cat shouldn't be crying like that," said the doctor. "That's not the ordinary cry of a cat who's angry at being shut in a basket. Let me have a look at her." He undid the cord that was holding the lid over the basket, and took out of it a black cat with blue-green eyes – just like your Ferry here – and, as he happened to notice when he was examining her closely, with three coarse white hairs under her chin.

'Then my ancestor gave a gentle little laugh and said, "What is wrong with this cat is that she had kittens a very short while ago, and why she's crying like this is because she's been taken away from her babies."

' "I didn't know she'd had kittens," said the boy in surprise. "It's true she's been off on her own a lot lately, but I thought it was because of the rough seas we'd been having just before we made port. I wonder where she can possibly have hidden them?"

' "We'll soon find out," said my ancestor the doctor. He put the cat Bessy back into the basket and tied it up again, and then they all set off for the *Unicorn*, the cat crying piteously all the way.

'As soon as they had crossed the gangplank on to the ship the boy let the cat out of the basket, and she was off like an arrow from a bow, the boy running swiftly after her, and the captain and the doctor panting along behind. The cat dodged along the deck, under the sailors' feet, running all out till she came to an old barrel that had once held fresh water and now lay empty on its side. Into the barrel dashed the cat, and when the captain and the doctor and the boy all jostled each other to peer in, what should they see there but four very tiny kittens, one black like the mother cat and three tiger-striped like the regular ship's cat Tibbs, all sprawled on the barrel staves with their eyes still shut.

'The captain and the doctor began to laugh and they laughed loud and long. Then the doctor turned to the boy. "With those kittens, my lad," he said, "you can step on to the first rung of the ladder of fortune and keep your Bessy as well. The kittens are far too young to leave their mother for quite a little while, but I expect the good captain will be in port for a few weeks yet?" He looked questioningly at Captain Fitzwarren, who said, "That I will, and longer than I meant to be. I had word this morning that the camel caravan which was bringing me a load of ivory from Timbuctoo has been delayed on the other side of the desert. But it's well worth my while to wait for it. Ivory fetches a high price in the markets of Europe."

' "Then what I suggest," said the doctor to the boy, "is that you bring your cat and her kittens and come and live with them in my kitchens until the *Unicorn* is ready to sail. In the meantime Bessy can make a start on the mice there and teach the kittens all they need to know, and I can promise you that my servants will see that all of you, cat and kittens and boy are thoroughly well fed –"

'The Captain broke in, "I'm all for your feeding my boy," he said. "He's a growing boy and it'll do him good to have a bit more to eat then he can get on a trading ship at sea. But you don't want to go feeding that cat, Doctor. Everyone knows that a full cat catches no mice."

' "Oh no, Captain," cried the boy. "I know that's true of some cats but not of Bessy. Truly, sir," he turned to the doctor, "the better you feed Bessy, the better she works. She's that kind of cat."

' "I can see that she is," said my ancestor firmly, and he went on, "When the kittens are grown and can be safely left behind, then I will pay you a fair price for them. You will be able to buy goods on the market here and sell them in the markets of England. Thus you will

have a good chance to begin to make your fortune and have your Bessy with you to enjoy it.''

'And so it happened. It was over two months before the camels from Timbuctoo plodded into Tangiers with the ivory on their backs. By that time the kittens were quite big enough to be parted from Bessy who, by then, had caught almost all the rats and mice in the doctor's house and had given the kittens such good lessons in the work that every one of them was capable of keeping a house free from vermin. The doctor paid the boy generously for the four kittens, and then one of the doctor's merchant-cousins helped the boy to buy the very best soft white cotton that he'd brought to Morocco from Smyrna. Off they sailed to London on the *Unicorn*, the cat and the boy and the captain, and when next Captain Fitzwarren put into Tangiers, he told the doctor that in London the boy had sold his cotton at such a good price that he had been able to buy himself an apprenticeship with the captain's brother who was a great London merchant. A few years later the captain told my ancestor that the boy had married his master's daughter and taken to trading on his own account, and on the very last voyage the captain made to Tangier, when he and my ancestor were both growing old, he said that the boy had grown into an important man who was honoured by the King of England. He had no more news of the cat Bessy, but we children who heard the story were always sure that she must have lived a happy cat life with her master until she died.'

*   *   *

Dr Nora finished her story and they all looked at Ferry lying stretched out on the rug, a cat who was just beginning a happy cat life with his own family. Then Rose got up and went into the kitchen and came back with a tray on which were glasses of fresh orange-juice and the Twelfth Day cake she had baked, a rich fruit cake with a dried bean hidden somewhere in it; and as Rose offered each person a slice, William told them of the old custom which is that whoever finds the bean in his slice is the Twelfth Day King. This time it was Brother Felix who found it, which was suitable, Epiphany being a Christian festival, and he the only Christian there.

As they were eating their cake and sipping their juice, Brother Felix said, 'Well, now we really do know, or think we know, the whole of Ferry's history. We know that he lived wild somewhere on the Jerusalem hillside, we believe that one of his ancestors may have come up to Jerusalem from Jaffa with one of our Franciscan brothers. We think it extremely likely that an even earlier ancestor came to Jaffa from Morocco with one of Dr Nora's merchant cousins, and we are nearly sure that an earlier ancestor still sailed to Morocco from England some 500 years ago. There are few humans whose family history can be traced back for such a long time and so completely.'

William said, 'We can trace Ferry's family history further back than that. There's still another story to tell.' He turned to Dr Nora and asked her, 'Did your ancestor's story give the name of the cabin-boy?'

'Why, yes, it did,' answered Dr Nora, puzzled by his question. 'The boy's name is a part of the story, but I left it out here because it doesn't make sense to me.'

'What is it?' William demanded.

Dr Nora said, 'Deek or Deekie or something like that.'

'Just as I thought!' William exclaimed. He looked around at the others. 'Of course you'll all have realised who the cabin-boy was,' he said. They looked blankly back at him. 'It was Dick Whittington, of course,' said William. 'Dick Whittington – you know, Richard Whittington.' Still their faces were uncomprehending, and William said impatiently, 'Every English child knows the story of Dick Whittington.'

'But, William,' Ezra said gently, 'no one here but yourself ever has been an English child. So it is you who must tell us this story.' The others nodded agreement, and William began:

*   *   *

'Since I'm the only Londoner here,' he said, 'as well as being the one from England, I must start by telling you that on a high hill to the north of London there is a village called Highgate: and there, as it happened, I was brought up, and there my parents live still. The village of Highgate has stood on that hill for a very long time, and for a longer time still the main road from the north has run onwards from Highgate Hill, steeply down into the very centre of old London. Nowadays there are houses and shops all along the road into London, but only a hundred years ago there were still some fields between London and Highgate, and five hundred years ago, when Dick Whittington began to trudge down that hill on sore tired feet, Highgate was just a little village, and between

Highgate and London there was nothing on that road but a few other little villages, and open country all around them.

'Dick Whittington had walked all the way from Gloucestershire, a shire which is a good hundred miles away from London in the West Country. His was a farming family but he was the third-born boy in it so he would have to make his own fortune, and he had decided to come to London to seek it there. He had often heard people say what a rich city London was, so rich, some said, that its streets were paved with gold; though

Dick, being a sensible boy, took that with a grain of salt and expected that even among London's streets some would be not of gold but of cobblestones, and often hard dirty cobblestones at that. But that London was rich no one denied, and young Dick was confident that for a boy who was ready to work hard and needed to make his own fortune, London was the right place to be.

'So he had set out from his home in Gloucestershire, with a few provisions to eat on the journey tied up in a bundle which he carried on the end of a stick. And with him he took what he loved most dearly in all the world,

his cat, whose name I know now – though I never knew before – was Bessy. I expect that for part of the long trudge to London he carried Bessy, and that for part of the way she trotted along beside him, as many a good cat does; even our timid Ferry will come with us for an evening stroll, so long as we don't go beyond the end of the street, and Sam Khan, the Abyssinian from a few doors away, goes for quite long walks with his master.

'But by the time Dick and Bessy had passed through Highgate Village they had walked a very long way. They were both of them tired and dusty and footsore and Dick, at least, was beginning to feel discouraged. The nearer they got to London, the less the people he met talked of London's streets being paved with gold, and the more they spoke of the hard dirty cobblestones, and of all the poor people and beggars in London who could find no work to do or food to eat. Utterly weary, Dick sat himself down on a milestone, a milestone which told the traveller that to the heart of London there were still four miles to go. And, equally weary, the cat, Bessy stretched out on the wayside grass beside her master, too tired even to eat her share of Dick's last crust of bread.

'Dick sighed deeply, and said to himself, "It's no good, I was a fool to think that I could make my fortune in London when everyone I meet tells me that so many people are starving there. I suppose there's nothing for it but to pick up Bessy and turn back north and then west again – if we're lucky, I'll pick up a job somewhere as a farmer's boy on the way."

'He stood up to take what he thought would be his last look southwards and as he looked, the early morning mist that had been shrouding the city dissolved before him, dried up by the rising sun. He saw before him London, its spires and steeples and towers all glittering in the sunlight. It was as beautiful as the London of his dreams and tears came to his eyes as he gazed on it, believing he must leave it behind him. Yet turn his back on it he must, he told himself, and resolutely he tucked his stick with its now nearly empty bundle under his arm, and was just about to pick up Bessy – when the bells of London's churches began to ring for Mattins. Ding-dong, they rang, ding-dong, ding-dong, high and low, sweet and harsh, jangled and harmonious, and as Dick listened, it seemed to him that one set of bells was raising its voice above the others, was speaking to him, especially to him, Dick Whittington the boy from Gloucestershire who was just about to turn his back on London for ever; and what these bells seemed to sing was:

> Turn again, Whittington, turn,
> Thrice Mayor of London town.

William broke off and said, 'The words really ought to be sung, but I'm rotten at singing.' Everyone said, 'Oh, do try,' and as he tried in a voice that was, as he'd said, not very tuneful, Ezra pulled out of his pocket the tiny flute he always carried with him. 'It should be like this, I think,' he said, and played the tune as it should be, the tune of the church bells:

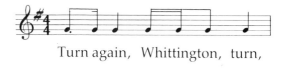

Turn again, Whittington, turn,

Thrice Mayor of London town.

To the tune as Ezra played it, they could all put the words that William had told them:

Turn again, Whittington, turn,
Thrice Mayor of London town.

and no one was surprised when William went on: 'For so long as the bells were ringing, Dick stood there listening. When they stopped, he turned his back on the north and set his face towards London again. "Come along, Bessy," he said in a newly strong voice, and determinedly he and his cat made their way southwards, down the Highgate Hill into London.

'Of course Dick found it hard at first, very hard indeed. As everyone had told him, there was no work to be found in London for a poor boy with no trade and a cat to keep. But he kept up his hopes and his spirits, and if ever he felt like losing them, he had only to listen to London's bells and especially to what he came to think of as his own bells, the bells of, as he learnt, the church of St Mary-le-Bow in Cheapside which daily promised him his fortune in London.

'But his fortune was a long time coming, and Dick and Bessy were, both of them, nearly on their last legs when Dick met the master of the *Unicorn*, and Captain Fitzwarren offered to take on boy and cat as cabin-boy and second ship's-mouser. What happened after Dick and Bessy arrived in Morocco, Dr Nora has told us; though I never knew before that his cat had kittens there, and that it was the kittens he sold there, not Bessy. As they tell the story in England, it's Dick's cat that he has to sell in Morocco, and when I was a little boy I used to cry at the thought that Dick Whittington and his cat had to part for ever.'

'And did Dick become Mayor of London?' Brother Felix asked.

'Indeed he did,' said William. 'Just as Captain Fitzwarren told Dr Nora's ancestor, Dick Whittington became a great merchant and a very rich man, so rich that even the King of England would borrow money from him. There's another story about him, not a long-told story this, but a written one, that after our King Henry V had dubbed Richard Whittington his knight, after he had in St Paul's Church tapped Dick on the shoulder with his sword and said, "Arise, Sir Richard", then the first toast the king called for at the banquet in the Guild Hall was "To the Cat!". And not once but three times, just as the bells had foretold, Sir Richard Whittington became Lord Mayor of London.

'And if,' William ended, 'one day when you are visiting England you leave London by way of the old north road, you will see, a little way up Highgate Hill on the left-hand side, a milestone where Dick Whittington stood and listened to the Bow Bells, and on the stone a statue of his cat, the great-great-hundreds-of-times great-grandmother of our cat Ferry.'

*   *   *

As William finished, Ferry woke up. Perhaps he had heard his name. He got to his feet and he stretched himself. Then he stalked through to the kitchen to see if he'd left any titbit in his meat saucer, though he knew perfectly well that he hadn't, for he always ate the best bits first. So he stalked back to the company and jumped on to Rose's lap, and Rose, for the first time, took up the new tortoiseshell toothbrush and brushed him between the ears, and at this, after a moment's silent surprise, he soon began purring with a very loud purr.

'That is really a fine cat,' said Ezra, 'a very fine cat indeed.'

'And with a fine ancestry,' agreed Brother Felix. Then he added in a worried voice, 'But what will become of Ferry when you go back to England or America, whichever it is you finally decide to go back to? It would be dreadful for the poor beast to have to return to a wild life after being so safe and happy here with you.'

'No call for that,' said Dr Nora firmly. 'If needs be I will gladly give Ferry a home, for his own sake and for his family's, but I think he would always be homesick now for this one.'

'No call for *that*,' said William. He looked at Rose and Rose looked at him. She said consideringly, 'Since Ferry came to us, we haven't had one single argument about where we are going to live.'

'But I think, in our hearts, we have decided,' said William. 'In fact, I am sure we have. We both know now that our home is here. Rose and I are going to go on living here in Jerusalem with our cat and our baby.'

'And with our Jakie's sister who will be born in a year or so and called Lucy for William's mother,' said Rose firmly. And so, in just over a year, it came to pass.

'And if,' finished William, 'if by any ill chance we should have to leave the land of Israel, then Ferry will come with us wherever we go.'

* * *

Whether William and Rose and their family leave or stay, only history will decide. Of one thing we can be sure, and this is that Ferry the Jerusalem Cat lived pretty well happy-ever-after. His humans, of course, did not, for to be happy-ever-after is not natural to humans and could never make for interesting lives. But they all lived as happily as anyone could reasonably expect or hope for.

The End